Archie in Strange change.

the Archie® DIGEST LIBRARY

Archie®

– in –

Strange Change

Spotlight

visit us at
www.abdopublishing.com

Exclusive Spotlight library bound edition published in 2007 by Spotlight, a division of ABDO Publishing Group, Edina, Minnesota. Spotlight produces high quality reinforced library bound editions for schools and libraries. Published by agreement with Archie Comic Publications, Inc.

Library of Congress Cataloging-in-Publication Data

Archie in Strange change / edited by Nelson Ribeiro & Victor Gorelick.
p. cm. -- (The Archie digest library)
Revision of issue no. 183 (Oct. 2001) of Archie digest magazine.
ISBN-13: 978-1-59961-262-1
ISBN-10: 1-59961-262-3
1. Comic books, strips, etc. I. Ribeiro, Nelson. II. Gorelick, Victor. III. Archie digest magazine. 183. IV. Title: Strange Change.

PN6728.A72A734 2007
741.5'973--dc22

2006049671

All Spotlight books are reinforced library binding and manufactured in the United States of America.

Contents

Archie®

UGH! A SCHOOL BUS? WHAT'S A SCHOOL BUS DOING ON THE ROAD *ALREADY*?
EASY, ARCHIE!
SCHOOL BUS
RIVERDALE HIGH SCHOOL
Archie® in "LESSON PLAN"
THE DRIVER IS PROBABLY MAKING A TEST RUN OF HER ROUTE! THE START OF SCHOOL IS JUST AROUND THE CORNER!
YOU DON'T HAVE TO REMIND ME! EVERYWHERE I LOOK I SEE SIGNS OF THAT DREADED DAY!

GROAN! SEE WHAT I MEAN!
BACK TO SCHOOL SALE 50% OFF!
GIANT BACK TO SCHOOL SALE! ON ALL SHOES!
IT'S NOT THAT I DON'T LIKE SCHOOL... IT'S JUST THAT I DON'T WANT TO BE REMINDED EVERY MINUTE THAT SUMMER VACATION IS ENDING!
I UNDERSTAND THAT, BUT I THINK YOU'RE MAKING A MOUNTAIN OUT OF A MOLE HIILL!
GLOOM!
OH, AM I?
I.M. LATE EMPLOYMENT AGENC
SCHOOL CROSSING GUARDS NEEDED IMMEDIATELY
GULP! WELL, JUST PUT SCHOOL OUT OF YOUR MIND AND ENJOY WHAT'S LEFT OF VACATION!
I'D LIKE TO!
2

BUT IT'S NOT EXACTLY THAT EASY!
I GUESS NOT!
STOP
RIVERDALE POLICE DEPT. REMINDS YOU THAT...
SCHOOL IS OPEN SO DRIVE CAREFULLY!
ALL YOU NEED IS TO GET AWAY FROM THIS SCHOOL HYPE FOR A WHILE!
RIGHT! AND HOW DO I DO THAT?
HMM...BIKE OUT INTO THE COUNTRY! THERE'S NOT MUCH TO REMIND YOU OF SCHOOL OUT IN THE BOONDOCKS!
HEY! NOW THAT IS A GOOD IDEA!
HOW ABOUT JOINING ME?
GEE, SORRY, ARCHIE I CAN'T! I HAVE TO GO SHOPPING!
SHOPPING? FOR WHAT?
WELL, - GULP! - SCHOOL CLOTHES! SEE YA!
3

BETTY SURE HAD A GREAT IDEA! THIS IS JUST WHAT I NEEDED TO FORGET ABOUT SCHOOL!
OUT HERE ALL I HAVE TO THINK ABOUT ARE THE BIRDS AND THE CLOUDS!
I DON'T HAVE A CARE IN THE WORLD... HUH?
KA POW!
SSSSSSSS
RATS! A BLOW OUT! AND I DON'T HAVE A REPAIR KIT!
IT'LL BE A LONG WALK BACK IF I CAN'T FLAG DOWN A RIDE! HEY! I'M IN LUCK, HERE COMES A CAR!
4

YO! PLEASE STOP! I NEED ASSISTANCE!
SCREECH!
THANKS FOR STOPPING TO HELP A STRANGER, MISTER!
100-76
I WOULDN'T EXACTLY CALL ONE OF MY STUDENTS A STRANGER!
GULP! MR. WEATHERBEE!
I'M ON MY WAY HOME FROM A FISHING TRIP! PUT YOUR BIKE IN THE TRUNK AND HOP IN!
YES, SIR! THANK YOU!
MINUTES LATER...
YOUR MISFORTUNE IS MY GOOD LUCK! NOW I'LL HAVE SOMEONE TO TALK TO DURING THE LONG DRIVE TO TOWN!
I'M SURE YOU'LL WANT TO HEAR ALL ABOUT MY PLANS FOR THE START OF THE NEW SCHOOL YEAR!
End

AHHH... NOW FOR ONE OF THE MOST RELAXING RITES OF WARM WEATHER!
Archie in "HAMMOCK ROCKY ROAD"

A SNOOZE IN THE OL' HAMMOCK!

UH-OH!
1

I FORGOT! I CAN'T PUT THE HAMMOCK IN IN THE OLD SPOT!

POP AND I CHOPPED DOWN THE OLD, DEAD TREE FOR FIREWOOD LAST FALL!

OH WELL, I'LL JUST HAVE TO FIND A NEW SHADY SPOT FOR ME AND MY HAMMOCK!

HEY! THAT LOOKS LIKE A GOOD PLACE!

I'LL JUST KNOT THE ROPES TO THESE SAPLINGS AND HOP ON!
2

HOP!
SPONG
HUMPH!

I GUESS THIS ISN'T GOING TO WORK!

I'LL HAVE TO FIND ANOTHER SPOT!
TWANG

WHOAA... MUCHO PROBLEMO!

NO OTHER TWO TREES IN OUR YARD ARE CLOSE ENOUGH TO HANG A HAMMOCK!

HEY! BUT IF I USE ONE OF OUR TREES AND ONE OF THE NEIGHBOR'S, IT MIGHT WORK!
3

THIS SHOULDN'T CAUSE A PROBLEM! MR. MARTIN IS VERY FRIENDLY!

AHH... NOW TO RELAX... H-HUH? WHAT THE...?
WHIRRR
PUTT-PUTT-PUTT!
SPRONG

YO, ARCHIE! THAT HAMMOCK HAS TO GO!
GULP! SURE, MR. MARTIN! I'LL MOVE IT RIGHT AWAY!
WHIRR!
PUTT! PUTT!

SORRY, ARCHIE! MAYBE WHEN I'M DONE YOU CAN PUT IT BACK UP!
THAT'S OKAY, SIR! I'LL FIND ANOTHER PLACE!
WHIRRR

BUT WHERE? I MIGHT AS WELL PUT THE HAMMOCK BACK IN THE GARAGE... HUH?
4

LATER...
I WONDER WHERE ARCHIE IS? I THOUGHT HE WAS GOING TO PUT UP THE HAMMOCK!

I DON'T SEE HIM ANYWHERE IN THE YARD!

WAIT A MINUTE! WHAT'S THAT LOUD NOISE? IT SOUNDS LIKE SNORING!
ZZZZZZZ

IT'S COMING FROM THERE!
ZZZZZZ

HUMPH! WELL, HOW DO YOU LIKE THAT!
ZZZZZZZZ
END

OKAY, ARCH! I'M READY!
VERONICA, WHY ARE YOU DRESSED LIKE THAT?
Veronica -IN- OUT OF CONTROL
I ALWAYS DRESS THIS WAY WHEN I GO TO THE BEACH!
EEP! YOU NEVER LISTEN! WHEN I CALLED, I SAID WE WERE GOING HIKING ON THE MOUNTAIN!
1

HA! YOU NEVER LISTEN! I SAID THE BEACH!

THERE YOU GO AGAIN! YOU ALWAYS HAVE TO GET YOUR WAY!!

HOLD IT! FLAG ON THE PLAY!
IT'S THE BEACH... OR IT'S NO DATE!

OKAY! OKAY! I SEE WE'RE ON A COLLISION COURSE AND I'M NOT BUDGING!

NEITHER AM I... SO GO TAKE A HIKE!
I WILL! HAVE A NICE DAY!
2

GRRR... SHE'S A CONTROL FREAK! BUT NOT THIS TIME, VERONICA!!

WHEN I SAY "TO GO HIKING"... I'M GOING HIKING! I'M NOT ALWAYS GOING TO GIVE IN!

HA! WHO NEEDS ARCHIE? I'LL CALL BETTY TO GO WITH ME!

HUMPH! NO ANSWER! GUESS I'M OFF TO THE BEACH ALL BY MYSELF!

I'M NOT GOING TO LET ARCHIE SPOIL MY DAY! SO WHY DO I KEEP THINKING ABOUT HIM?

WHOA, GIRL! LOOK OVER THERE... W-WHY IT'S ARCHIE!
3

HA! I KNEW THE SILLY BOY WOULD COME AROUND!

HUH? YOU'RE NOT ARCHIE!
NO, CUTIE! BUT WON'T I DO?

NO THANK YOU!! GO TAKE A SWIM TO COOL OFF, BUSTER!!
SMACK!

HUMPH! I CAN'T HELP IT... BUT I CAN'T STOP THINKING OF ARCHIE...

EVERY PLACE HERE REMINDS ME OF THE TIMES I CAME HERE WITH HIM!
SNACK
SNACKS

I REMEMBER THE FIRST TIME HE BOUGHT ME A TRIPLE SCOOP!
4

LOOK OUT, LADY!!
?
CLUNK!
SPLAT!

SORRY, LADY! HEE-HEE!

EEPS! I'M A MESS! I'VE GOT TO WASH THIS GOOK OFF WITH A SWIM!
5

OW!
A CRAB!
I'VE HAD IT!
I'M OUT OF HERE!

GRRR... WHAT A DAY! A BUMMER! JUST A BAD BEACH DAY!

HI, BETTY! GOOD, YOU'RE HOME AT LAST-- TRIED TO CALL YOU BEFORE!
OH, I WAS OUT HIKING AND GUESS WHO I RAN INTO...

...FUNNY! SHE GUESSED IT WAS ARCHIE AND THEN WE WERE CUT OFF!

SCREAM!
LODGE
END

Mr. Weatherbee
in
"A WEIGHTY MATTER"
MR. WEATHERBEE, THIS IS A SURPRISE! I NEVER THOUGHT I'D RUN INTO YOU AT THE FAIR!
I'M TRYING TO RELAX AND GET MY MIND OFF MY TROUBLES!
HOT DOGS - HAMBURGERS
CUSTARD
SODA
TROUBLES?! WHAT TROUBLES?
LAST JUNE THE SUPERINTENDENT SENT OUT A WARNING ABOUT PRINCIPALS BEING OVERWEIGHT!

I'VE TRIED DIETING AND EXERCISING, BUT NOTHING SEEMS TO WORK!
...I COULD LOSE MY JOB THIS SEPTEMBER!

LET'S GO, AUNTY!
GOOD LUCK!
I'LL NEED MORE THAN LUCK!
1

LOOK! THERE'S MR. WEATHERBEE!
DRAT! THERE'S ARCHIE! HE'S THE LAST PERSON I WANT TO SEE AT A TIME LIKE THIS!

I DON'T THINK HE SEES US, JUG!
I'LL JUST DUCK IN HERE FOR THE TIME BEING!
FUN
HOUSE
ADMISSI

THIS IS MOST CONFUSING!

OH, NO!

HOW DO I FIND MY WAY OUT OF THIS CRAZY PLACE?

KRASH!
2

AH! AN EXIT AT LAST!

I BETTER DUCK INTO THIS LONG LINE UNTIL HE PASSES!
HE AND I MUST HAVE JUST MISSED EACH OTHER!

HOW MANY TICKETS, JACK?
"HOW MANY"?
$1.50 A RIDE

I GUESS YOU WANT SIX!
WHA?

?? WHERE ARE WE GOING?

LET ME STRAP YOU IN, SIR!
GOOD GRIEF! I SEEM TO HAVE GOTTEN ON SOME KIND OF RIDE!
RIDE AT YOUR OWN RISK
FASTEN SEAT BELTS PLEASE!

OH NO!
3

EEAGHH!!

THAT PLUCKY OL' GUY IS STICKING AROUND FOR MORE RIDES!

OH, NO! I'M STILL ON THIS MANIACAL CONTRAPTION!

ONE HALF HOUR LATER -
HOW I SURVIVED, I'LL NEVER KNOW!

LOOK, IT'S MR. WEATHERBEE!
IT'S ARCHIE AGAIN!

DARN! I RAN INTO A BLIND ALLEY!

IF I CAN JUST HOP OVER THIS FENCE I'LL BE OKAY!
FAIR RODEO
BIG PRIZES
4

WHAT THE ?...

YOU MUST BE THE GUY THEY SENT TO HELP ME CHASE THE BULLS AWAY FROM THE RIDERS WHO FALL!
'BULLS'?!

YIPES!!!

THAT NEW FELLOW IS WORKING OUT JUST FINE!
EEEEOOOOOW!

WHEW! I THOUGHT I'D NEVER GET OUT OF THERE!
MR. WEATHERBEE! MR. WEATHERBEE!

ARCHIE, WILL YOU STOP HOUNDING ME ?
I JUST WANTED TO SAY "HELLO"!

GULP! I'M SORRY!
5

GUESS YOUR WEIGHT, SIR?
HUH?

I'D SAY YOU WERE ABOUT 225!
OF COURSE! I WEIGH 225!

I WAS WRONG! YOU'RE ONLY 212!
GOOD HEAVENS! I LOST 13 POUNDS... WHILE I WAS TRYING TO AVOID ARCHIE!

ARCHIE! COME BACK!
HEY! DON'T YOU WANT YOUR PRIZE?

ARCHIE, I OWE YOU AN APOLOGY! YOU SAVED ME MY JOB!
WHA-?

KEEP FEEDING THEM AND DON'T STOP UNTIL THEY BOTH SHOUT "MERCY"!
GEE! AND I THOUGHT GIRLS WERE DIFFICULT TO UNDERSTAND!
1.75
The END 6

Archie in "CAR TROUBLE"

I DON'T CARE! IF THIS GOOF IS BEHIND THE WHEEL, HE'LL FIND SOME WAY TO FOUL IT UP!

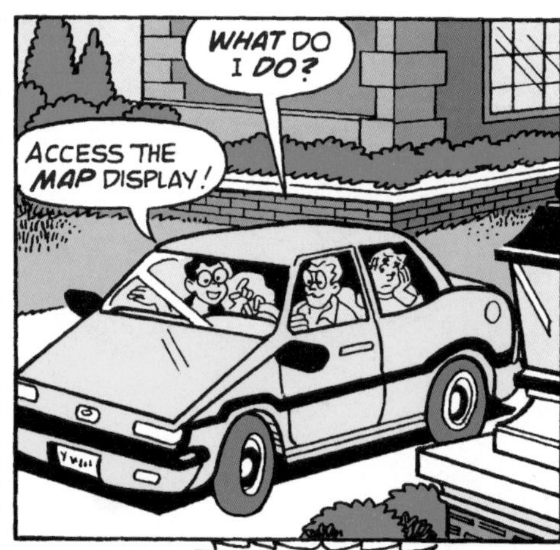
WHAT DO I DO?
ACCESS THE MAP DISPLAY!

NOW WHAT?
SCROLL THE MAP FOR YOUR DESTINATION THEN PRESS "ACTIVATE"!

"ACTIVATED"!
IS THIS THING SAFE?
TOTALLY!

IT FINDS ITS WAY BY BOUNCING SIGNALS OFF A SATELLITE...
FASTEN YOUR SEAT BELTS!

AND IT OBEYS ALL TRAFFIC REGULATIONS...
SPEED LIMIT 25 MPH!
2

PEDESTRIAN CROSSING! MUST YIELD RIGHT OF WAY!

IT REACTS TO EMERGENCIES FASTER THAN A HUMAN DRIVER CAN!

THERE IS CONSTRUCTION BLOCKING ELM ST.

WE WILL DETOUR VIA 12TH ST., SPRUCE ST. AND 8TH ST.!
MARVELOUS!

HOW DOES IT KNOW THAT?
IT ACCESSES THE CITY DATA BASE!

SCHOOL ZONE SLOW TO 15 MPH, TRAFFIC LIGHT AMBER MUST SLOW TO STOP!
WE CAN MAKE A FORTUNE WITH THIS CAR!
SCHOOL ZONE
3

SPEED LIMIT 85!
WHAT?!

RIGHT TURN!
THIS IS A ONE-WAY STREET!
ONE WAY

DILTON, WHAT'S GOING ON?
I DON'T KNOW!
EEEEEK!
WORLD

ISN'T THERE A MANUAL OVERRIDE?
IT'S NOT FUNCTIONING!

THERE'S SOME KIND OF ELECTRONIC INTERFERENCE! IT'S THE ELECTRONIC GAME!
BEEP BEEP

ARCHIE, SHUT OFF THAT ELECTRONIC GAME! QUICK!
BEEP
BEEP
BEEP
4

THAT WAS THE PROBLEM! THE MANUAL OVERRIDE IS ENGAGED!
SCREEECH!
IT'S TOO LATE! EVERYBODY, BRACE YOURSELVES!
KA-BAM!
P.D
PD
ER... GOOD MORNING, OFFICER!
EVEN THOUGH HE WAS BEHIND THE WHEEL WHEN ARRESTED, MR. LODGE CLAIMED HE WASN'T DRIVING!
POLICE DEPT.
14TH PRECINCT
CBJ TV
CBJ TV
END

GET SET FOR ANOTHER GREAT STORY WITH ME BACK WHEN I WAS KNOWN AS...
Little Archie

CHIEF McNAB
PARKER PENBINDER
CALEB WARFIELD
Little Archie
JIMMY LEE
MAYOR MALLET
TONI GREENWOOD
R
SWAMP
N
E
THE STRANGE CASE OF THE MYSTERY MAP
DAWN IN RIVERDALE IS HERALDED BY THE THUMP OF THE MORNING PAPER THROWN AGAINST THE DOOR...
THERE ARE FEW HOMES IN TOWN THAT DO NOT SUBSCRIBE TO THE RIVERDALE RECORD...ONE IS THE HOME OF CALEB WARFIELD. IN FACT, THERE HAVE BEEN NO NEWSPAPERS DELIVERED TO THE WARFIELD ESTATE FOR TWENTY YEARS.
1

FUBLEY'S
ANTIQUES
YEAH, THAT'S THE PLACE. MA FUBLEY'S ANTIQUE SHOP.
BUT SHAKEY, WHY STICK UP OLD MA FUBLEY?

EVERYONE KNOWS MA FUBLEY DOESN'T TRUST BANKS, AND THE RUMOR'S OUT THAT SHE HAS FIVE GRAND STASHED AWAY SOME-WHERE IN HER STORE.

INSIDE THE STORE, MA FUBLEY HAS JUST MADE A SALE...
GLAD TO GET RID OF THIS OLD DIARY..I NEVER COULD READ ITS FAINT SCRIBBLE...NOT WITH MY WEAK EYES.

ALRIGHT, MA FUBLEY! THIS IS A STICKUP!
GLORY BE! A FIREARM!

MEANWHILE, NEXT DOOR...
IT'S SURE NICE OF YOU TO SHOW ME AROUND THE NEWSPAPER AND TEACH ME ALL ABOUT CAMERAS TOO, JIMMY.
I MAY BE JUST AN OFFICE BOY FOR THE RIVER-DALE RECORD NOW, BUT SOME DAY I'M GOING TO BE ITS STAR REPORTER!
2

LET'S GET BACK ON MY MOTORBIKE AND GET THESE COFFEES TO THE MEN IN THE PRESS ROOM.
SPEAKING OF CAMERAS, LOOK AT THIS OLD ONE IN THE WINDOW.

YEAH, IT'S—
HEY! WHAT'S GOING ON IN THERE?!

FREEZE, GRANDMAW, AND YOU'LL BE IN THE CLEAR!
MERCY! I'M GOING TO FAINT!

HEY, SHAKEY! THIS OLD BABE IS KEELING OV—

3

LADY! I CAN'T BELIEVE IT! WE LOOKED IN THE WINDOW IN TIME TO SEE YOU THROW THOSE TWO THUGS!
NOT A BAD WORKOUT... BUT MY TIMING WAS A MITE OFF WITH THE FLESHY FELLA.

MY NAME IS JIMMY LEE! I WORK FOR THE RIVERDALE RECORD! I'M GOING TO BE A REPORTER AND...
NEWSPAPERS! OH, DEAR! GOODBYE, YOUNG MAN!
4

GOOD DAY, BOYS!
WAIT! I HAVE A CAMERA THERE ON MY MOTOR BIKE!

HOW ABOUT A PICTURE AND A STORY ON YOU ?! WHEN THE EDITOR, MISTER PENBINDER, SEES IT-HE'S SURE TO PROMOTE ME!

(GROAN) THEY KEEP FOLLOWING ME...
MISSES DRESSES

AW, LADY! JUST A SHORT INTERVIEW ?!
DON'T JOSTLE ME, JUNIOR, IT'S TOO WARM IN HERE!
LADIES FITTING ROOM

WARM IS RIGHT, LADY! YOU'RE MELTING!

LADIES FITTING ROOM

SHE MUST COME OUT AND WHEN SHE DOES, I'LL TAKE A PICTURE OF HER, IN OR OUT OF DISGUISE!
LADIES FITTING ROOM
BUT HOW'LL YOU RECOGNIZE HER IF SHE'S OUT OF DISGUISE?
16 95

HER PERFUME! THAT WAY-OUT PERFUME! I'D NEVER FORGET IT!

(SNIFF) (SNIFF) NOPE!
(SNIFF)

SEVERAL SNIFFS LATER...
THAT'S HER! WOW! WHAT A DOLL!

SAY! WHAT'S THIS OLD LADY BIT ?!?

CAB!
WAIT!
TAXI

CONTINUED

C'MON! WE'LL FOLLOW HER ON MY MOTOR BIKE! WE CAN'T LET A STORY LIKE THIS GET AWAY!!
COFFEE

THEY PURSUE THE CAB, BUT OUT IN THE COUNTRYSIDE, THE DISTANCE BETWEEN THEM BECOMES GREATER...
THERE! ON THE SECOND CURVE! SHE'S HOPPED OUT OF THE CAB AND IS RUNNING TOWARD THE RIVER!!

ON ROUNDING A CURVE, THE BOYS MOMENTARILY LOSE SIGHT OF THE GIRL...

HERE'S HER TRACKS AND—HOLY SMOKES! SHE MUST'VE RUN RIGHT INTO THE RIVER!
THERE'S NO SIGHT OF HER!

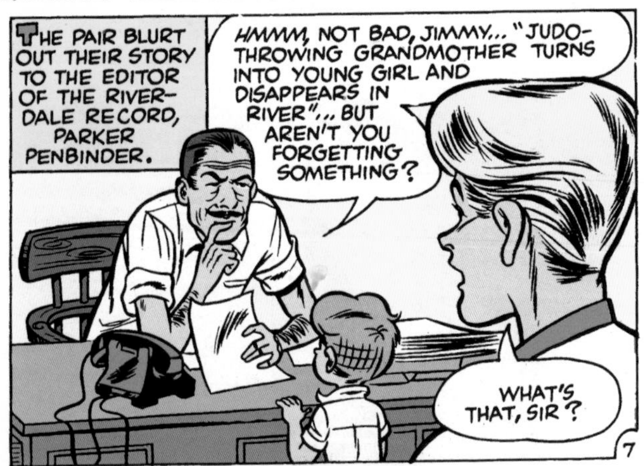
THE PAIR BLURT OUT THEIR STORY TO THE EDITOR OF THE RIVERDALE RECORD, PARKER PENBINDER.
HMMM, NOT BAD, JIMMY... "JUDO-THROWING GRANDMOTHER TURNS INTO YOUNG GIRL AND DISAPPEARS IN RIVER"... BUT AREN'T YOU FORGETTING SOMETHING?
WHAT'S THAT, SIR?
7

THE COFFEE!! YOU TEENAGE WEDGEHEAD!! YOU WENT FOR IT AN HOUR AGO!!
GOLLY! WE LEFT 'EM ON THE SIDEWALK!

GO DO SOME ERRANDS! ANYTHING! I'VE NO TIME FOR YOUR SUPERNATURAL MYSTERIES!

THIS WOULD BE A GREAT STORY IF WE COULD GET TO THE BOTTOM OF IT!
WHY WOULD A YOUNG GIRL DRESS UP AS AN OLD LADY? WHY?

MEANWHILE, THE YOUNG GIRL, ALIAS THE OLD LADY, HURRIES, WET AND DRIPPING, ALONG A DIMLY LIT PASSAGEWAY... SHE STOPS, PRESSES A CERTAIN ROCK AND—

AH! MISS GREENWOOD! YOU'RE UNCLE WAS BECOMING CONCERNED!
WHRRRRRR
JARVIS, I'VE BEEN HAVING A BALL! NOW WHERE IS UNCLE?

IN THE WEST GYM WITH MISTER ITO!
OH, YES, I CAN HEAR THE THUDS!
8

UNCLE!

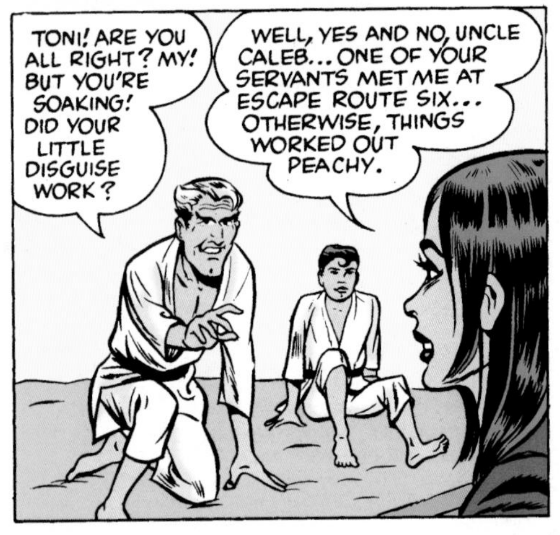
TONI! ARE YOU ALL RIGHT? MY! BUT YOU'RE SOAKING! DID YOUR LITTLE DISGUISE WORK?
WELL, YES AND NO, UNCLE CALEB... ONE OF YOUR SERVANTS MET ME AT ESCAPE ROUTE SIX... OTHERWISE, THINGS WORKED OUT PEACHY.

THEN YOU'VE GOT IT!?
YES! HERE IN THE WATERPROOF BAG. YOUR HUNCH WAS RIGHT. MA FUBLEY HAD IT ON A BACK SHELF.

AT LAST! AT LAST! COME TO MY STUDY WHEN YOU'VE DRIED OFF!
YOU WISH TO PRACTICE YOUR JUDO, MISS TONI?
NO THANKS, MISTER ITO. I'VE JUST HAD MY WORK-OUT.

LATER
WELL, UNCLE CALEB, DOES THE DIARY HELP?
MOST REVEALING MY DEAR, HEE! HEE!
9

THIS OLD DIARY THAT'S TAKEN SO LONG TO TRACE, IS IT GOING TO LEAD US INTO ANOTHER ONE OF OUR CRAZY ADVENTURES?
MORE THAN THAT, TONI. THERE'S GOING TO BE REAL **TREASURE** IN THIS ADVENTURE!

OH, UNCLE! YOU NEED MONEY LIKE YOU NEED THE MEASLES!
THIS DIARY WE'VE BEEN HUNTING IS RIGHTFULLY OURS!! IT WAS THE PERSONAL LOG OF OUR PIRATICAL ANCESTOR, CAPTAIN JONAH LASHMAST!

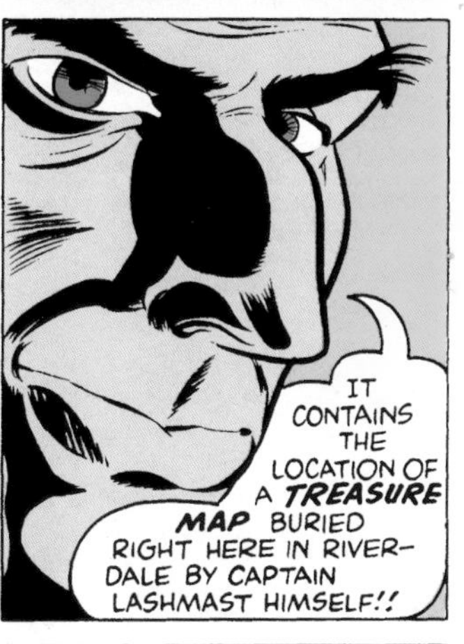
IT CONTAINS THE LOCATION OF A **TREASURE MAP** BURIED RIGHT HERE IN RIVERDALE BY CAPTAIN LASHMAST HIMSELF!!

BUT SOMETHING HAS HAPPENED I WAS AFRAID MIGHT **OCCUR**!!
WHAT'S THAT?

I CHECKED OUT CAPTAIN LASHMAST'S DIRECTIONS WITH THESE NEW GEODETIC SURVEY MAPS AND I'VE PINPOINTED THE EXACT LOCATION OF THE BURIED TREASURE MAP.
THEN, WHAT'S WRONG?

THE TREASURE MAP IS BURIED RIGHT UNDER THE RIVERDALE CITY HALL!
10

OH, UNCLE! IF WE WENT TO MAYOR MALLET AND TOLD HIM ABOUT IT I'M SURE—
WHAT!?!! AND HAVE HIM BLAB IT TO THE INFERNAL NEWSPAPERS!?! YOU KNOW HOW I DESPISE NEWSPAPERS!

I HAVEN'T HAD A NEWSPAPER IN THIS HOUSE IN TWENTY YEARS! THOSE SNOOPY REPORTERS WERE ALWAYS PUBLICIZING MY HUSH-HUSH BUSINESS DEALS.
YES, I'VE HEARD YOU TELL HOW THEY FOUND OUT ABOUT YOUR AFRICAN DIAMOND MINE AND-

LOST A COOL MILLION ON THAT DEAL, I DID!
THE PAPERS HAVE BEEN TRYING TO GET A STORY AND PICTURES OF YOU FOR TWENTY YEARS!

HEE! SEEMS LIKE THE ONLY FUN I GET OUT OF LIFE ARE THESE LITTLE ADVENTURES AND DODGING NEWSPAPER REPORTERS!
I'VE ALWAYS ENJOYED THESE ADVENTURES WITH YOU, UNCLE, BUT THIS ONE IS TOO MUCH! HOW CAN WE EVER DIG UP A MAP THAT'S BURIED UNDER CITY HALL?

LISTEN CLOSELY, TONI, HERE'S MY PLAN... HEE! HEE!

LATE THAT NIGHT JIMMY IS AWAKENED FROM A SOUND SLEEP BY—
RRRRRRRRRR
POLICE SIRENS! A LOT OF 'EM!

RRRRRRRRR
GUESS I'LL TROT ON DOWN TO POLICE HEADQUARTERS!
CONTINUED
11

NEXT MORNING
IS JIMMY HOME, MRS. LEE?
THAT BOY! UP HALF THE NIGHT, HE WAS! NOW HE'S RUN OFF TO WORK WITHOUT DRINKING HIS COCOA!

LATER...
HEY, JIMMY! WHAT'S HAPPENING?
PLENTY, LITTLE ARCHIE, AND IT'S ALL ABOUT THE STORY WE'VE BEEN WORKING ON!
RIVERDALE RECORD

AN OLD LADY AND A MAN WERE SEEN RUNNING OUT OF CITY HALL LAST NIGHT! THE POLICE WERE CALLED BUT THEY COULDN'T CATCH THEM!
HOW'S THIS CONNECT WITH OUR CASE?

THE OLD LADY DROPPED A PERFUMED HANDKERCHIEF! POLICE CHIEF McNAB GAVE ME A WHIFF OF IT AND—
YOU MEAN..

RIGHT! IT WAS THE SAME PERFUME AS WORN BY OUR RIVER NYMPH!
WOW! WHAT DO YOU THINK SHE WAS UP TO?

(SIGH) DUNNO! I'VE BEEN THINKING ABOUT IT 'TIL I'M DIZZY. HOW'S ABOUT GOING FISHING IN MY BOAT THIS AFTERNOON? I ALWAYS THINK BETTER WITH A POLE IN MY HAND.
SWELL! AND I KNOW JUST WHERE WE OUGHT TO FISH!
12

THAT AFTERNOON . . .
OVER THERE! THAT'S THE SPOT WHERE THE GIRL DISAPPEARED!
SOMETIMES I WONDER IF SHE REALLY DID GO IN THE WATER,,, SHE COULD'VE DOUBLED BACK, Y'KNOW.

LET'S ANCHOR BY ONE OF THE WARFIELD FALLS,,, THERE'S ALWAYS BASS THERE.
I SURE WOULD LIKE TO FISH ABOVE THOSE FALLS BUT OLD MAN WARFIELD'S SERVANTS WOULD RUN US OFF.

I'VE HEARD THAT MISTER WARFIELD IS SOME KIND OF A RICH NUT WHO NEVER HAS HIS PICTURE IN THE PAPER.
WHEN YOU HAVE A FORTUNE, YOU'RE NOT A RICH NUT, YOU'RE AN ECCENTRIC MILLIONAIRE.

LATER...
GOT ONE!?
NO! DARN IT! CAUGHT ON THE BOTTOM,,, MY BEST LURE, TOO!

I'M GOING TO DIVE FOR IT. I HAVE SOME EXTRA SKIN DIVING GEAR UP FORWARD,,, HOW ABOUT A DIP?
GOOD IDEA!
13

GOT IT!
JIMMY! JIMMY! LOOK AT WHAT I'VE FOUND!

A FEW DIVES LATER...
SO THAT'S HOW IT'S DONE! PRETTY CLEVER, HUH?
LET'S HEAD BACK RIGHT NOW AND FIX THIS BOAT UP! THEN WE'LL BE READY FOR 'EM!
WHAT DID LITTLE ARCHIE DISCOVER? HOW WILL THEY "FIX" THE BOAT?

MEANWHILE, NOT FAR FROM THE RIVER, THE ECCENTRIC MILLION-AIRE AND HIS NIECE, TONI GREENWOOD, ARE PORING OVER MAPS...
HEE! MARVELOUS! THE OLD "WARFIELD LUCK" IS RUNNING HIGH!

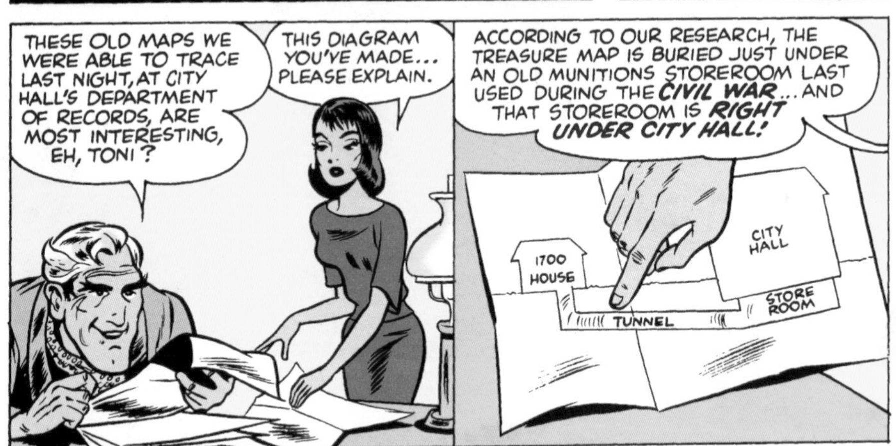
THESE OLD MAPS WE WERE ABLE TO TRACE LAST NIGHT, AT CITY HALL'S DEPARTMENT OF RECORDS, ARE MOST INTERESTING, EH, TONI?
THIS DIAGRAM YOU'VE MADE... PLEASE EXPLAIN.
ACCORDING TO OUR RESEARCH, THE TREASURE MAP IS BURIED JUST UNDER AN OLD MUNITIONS STOREROOM LAST USED DURING THE CIVIL WAR... AND THAT STOREROOM IS RIGHT UNDER CITY HALL!
1700 HOUSE
CITY HALL
STORE ROOM
TUNNEL

THIS AREA SUFFERED HEAVY CANNONADING DURING THE WAR AND THERE IS ONLY ONE TUNNEL THAT WASN'T DESTROYED...

THE ONE BENEATH THE TOWN SQUARE! IT CONNECTS THE STORE-ROOM TO THE OLD 1700 HOUSE... AND THAT'S WHERE WE GAIN ACCESS TO THE TUNNEL!
BUT THE 1700 HOUSE HAS BEEN LEFT STANDING SINCE THE AMERICAN REVOLUTION... IT'S BEEN ON EXHIBIT SINCE 1866! IT'S GUARDED!!

—AND I KNOW THERE ARE POLICE AROUND THE TOWN SQUARE AT NIGHT, TONI, BUT I'M CERTAIN WE CAN GO RIGHT INTO THAT HIDDEN TUNNEL IN BROAD DAYLIGHT. TOMORROW!
UNCLE! THEY'LL BE TOO MANY PEOPLE AROUND!
PRECISELY! AREN'T YOU FORGETTING WHAT TOMORROW IS?
OH, YES. RIVERDALE'S OBSERVANCE OF THAT GREAT CIVIL WAR BATTLE FOUGHT HERE. THE BATTLE OF RUTHLESS RIDGE.
ALL OF RIVERDALE WILL TURN OUT TO SEE THE CIVIL WAR PARADE AND HEAR MAYOR MALLET'S SPEECH.
I UNDERSTAND MAYOR MALLET HIMSELF WILL LEAD THE PARADE DRESSED AS GENERAL RANSOM RANKLE, HERO OF RUTHLESS RIDGE... BUT HOW WILL ALL THIS HELP US?
WHILE THE ENTIRE CROWD IS LISTENING TO MALLET, WE CAN SLIP UNSEEN INTO THE TUNNEL, FIND OUR WAY INTO THE STORE-ROOM, DIG UP THE MAP AND EXIT THE SAME WAY ALL DURING THE SPEECH.
WELL, MAYOR MALLET IS QUITE LONG-WINDED!
NEXT DAY...
WOW! WE CAN SEE EVERYTHING FROM HERE, JIMMY!... LOOKS LIKE A WHOLE CIVIL WAR ARMY DOWN THERE AROUND CITY HALL!
YEAH... AND MISTER PENBINDER TOLD ME TO GET SOME GOOD SHOTS OF THE PARADE.
CONTINUED
16

THIS ZOOM LENS ON YOUR MOVIE CAMERA IS GREAT! JUST LIKE A TELESCOPE!
MAYOR MALLET WILL SPEAK BEFORE THE PARADE AND IT LOOKS AS THOUGH HE'S GOING TO BEGIN.

I CAN SEE EVERYTHING SO CLEARLY... THEY'RE ALL LISTENING TO THE MAYOR.. WELL *ALMOST* EVERYONE... THIS MAN AND GIRL ARE HEADING FOR THE 1700 HOUSE AND—

HOLY SMOKES! IT'S HER! THE YOUNG GIRL! I MEAN THE OLD LADY— I MEAN—
HUH!? GIVE ME THAT!

1700 HOUSE
VISITING HOURS

IT *IS* HER! C'MON, LITTLE ARCHIE, LET'S SEE WHAT SHE'S UP TO!

YOU WERE RIGHT, UNCLE,.. NOBODY NOTICED US!

HERE! HERE IN THE CLOSET FLOOR! THE TUNNEL ENTRANCE... HELP ME PRY IT UP.
CREAK

LOOKS AS THOUGH THIS TUNNEL HASN'T BEEN USED IN YEARS!
NOT SINCE THE CIVIL WAR, TONI!

SHORTLY...
THIS IS IT! THE STOREROOM! NOW IF MY CALCULATIONS ARE CORRECT WE SHOULD DIG TWELVE PACES FROM THE SOUTHWEST CORNER!

ACCORDING TO CAPTAIN LASHMAST'S DIARY, THE MAP IS IN A BOTTLE.
THERE'S SOME OLD CIVIL WAR UNIFORMS HANGING HERE.

MEANWHILE...
WHERE'S THE GUARD THAT'S SUPPOSED TO BE HERE?
I SAW HIM ON THE CITY HALL STEPS, LISTENING TO MAYOR MALLET.
1700 HOUSE

HA!

GEE! IT'S DARK DOWN HERE!
SHHH! LIGHT UP AHEAD!

WHAT'RE THEY DOING?
DIGGING!

WHO IS THAT MAN?
NEVER SAW HIM, BUT I'M GOING TO FLASH A PICTURE OF HIM AND THEN WE'LL HIGHTAIL IT OUT OF HERE!

AH! EXACTLY AS THE DIARY SAID!
AND HERE'S THE MAP ROLLED UP INSIDE!

CLINK
CLINK
19

OH, NO! IT'S THAT BOY FROM THE NEWSPAPER.. AGAIN!!
DID I EVER TELL YOU ABOUT MY CAMERA-SHY UNCLE ?!
YEOW
STOP YELLING! THIS IS THE SOFTEST THROW I KNOW!
I HAVE THE MAP, TONI! GRAB A UNIFORM AND LET'S GET OUT OF HERE!
CALEB WARFIELD AND HIS NIECE RACE OUT OF THE TUNNEL WHILE, UP ABOVE, MAYOR MALLET DRONES ENDLESSLY ON ABOUT THE BATTLE OF RUTHLESS RIDGE...
THEN OUR GALLANT, BUT OUT-NUMBERED, FORCES RALLIED AND REPULSED THE ENEMY'S ATTACK—
20

SUDDENLY, THE CROWD'S ATTENTION IS FOCUSED ON RIVERDALE'S MOST PROMINENT BANKER, WALDO P. COPPERCLUTCH.
MY WALLET'S GONE!! SOMEONE'S PICKED MY POCKET!!

THE NEWS SPREADS QUICKLY THROUGH THE THRONG...
BANKER COPPERCLUTCH HAS BEEN ROBBED!
HE'S BEEN ROBBED!
WHO?
THE BANKER!

BANK ROBBERS!!
THE BANK'S BEEN ROBBED!

AT THAT MOMENT, CALEB AND TONI EMERGE INTO THE SUNLIGHT...
HURRY! THEY'RE RIGHT BEHIND US.
QUICKLY! PUT ON YOUR HAT AND COAT!

NOW TO LOSE OURSELVES IN THE CROWD..

WAIT! I'VE A MORE EXCITING IDEA!!
21

HORSE OWNER, MORGAN FETLOCK, TURNS IN TIME TO SEE TWO OF HIS FINEST PARADE MOUNTS MOVING OFF.
STOP! THIEF!

BUT THE CRY IS MISUNDERSTOOD...
THERE THEY GO! THERE GO THE BANK ROBBERS!

THE CAVALRY SQUAD THAT WAS TO HAVE RIDDEN IN THE PARADE IS COMPOSED MOSTLY OF POLICEMEN. THEY QUICKLY MOUNT AND GIVE CHASE.

MAYOR MALLET LEADS THEM..
ONCE MORE OUR GALLANT FORCES RALLY!

THERE THEY GO!
1700
WOW! LOOKS AS THOUGH THE WHOLE TOWN'S AFTER EM!
22

THEY'RE HEADED FOR THE RIVER!
GOOD! YOU KNOW WHAT WE HAVE TO DO!

THE SQUAD CAR ON DUTY FINDS PASSING IMPOSSIBLE ON THE ONLY ROAD TO THE RIVER...
POLI

LITTLE ARCHIE AND JIMMY LEE ARE ALSO HEADED FOR THE RIVER... BY A TWISTING, TREACHEROUS, BUT LESS CROWDED ROUTE.

UNCLE! I CAN HEAR THEM CALLING US BANK ROBBERS! MAYBE WE'D BETTER STOP AND EXPLAIN!
NO!! NEVER! THE INFERNAL NEWSPAPERS WOULD GET MY NAME AND PICTURE! PRESS ON TO THE RIVER! ITO WILL BE THERE!

THE RIVER!
—AND THERE'S ITO! I TOLD HIM TO STAND BY... JUST IN CASE!!
CONTINUED

GOOD TO SEE YOU, ITO! THE HOUNDS ARE NIPPING AT OUR HOCKS!

LOOK! THEIR MOUNTS! THEY MUST BE HERE... SPREAD OUT, I SAY!

MAYOR MALLET, REMEMBER *I'M* THE POLICE CHIEF!
PLEASE, McNAB! WOULD YOU MIND CALLING ME "GENERAL" 'TILL THIS IS OVER?! OTHERWISE, IT COULD BE BAD FOR MORALE!

LISTEN, MALLET, THE GAME *IS* OVER! WE'RE AFTER *REAL* BANK ROBBERS AND I'M IN CHARGE!
I'LL HAVE YOU COURT-MARTIALED FOR THIS, McNAB!

SPREAD OUT, MEN!
I'VE ALREADY GIVEN THAT ORDER!

SHORTLY
NOT A SIGN OF THEM, CHIEF!
LET THEM SLIP THROUGH YOUR FINGERS, HEY, McNAB?
24

HMMM.. "DISAPPEARS INTO RIVER"... YOUNG LEES CRAZY TALE...NOT SO FANTASTIC NOW...(GROAN) THAT KID MIGHT HAVE HAD A STORY AND I TURNED HIM AWAY...
KRAAAAAAWW
WHAT'S THAT RACKET?
LOOK! THE RIVER!
IT'S JIMMY LEE IN HIS OUTBOARD!
GOT 'ER WIDE OPEN, HE HAS!
WHO'S THAT RED HEADED YOUNG 'UN WITH HIM?
THE ANDREWS BOY! LITTLE ARCHIE!
THEY'RE HEADED STRAIGHT FOR THE FALLS!
THEY'LL BE KILLED!
25

GET UNDER THE TARP, LITTLE ARCHIE! HERE WE GO!!

KKKKKKK(SPUT)KKRRRAAAAAAAWWMMM
26

HOLD IT RIGHT THERE!
UNCLE, MEET JIMMY LEE OF THE RIVERDALE RECORD!
(GASP) A-A- NEWSPAPER!
ONE MORE FOR THE CENTER SECTION!
SAY CHEESE!
BUT-BUT- HOW—DID— WHERE (GASP)!!
IT HAD TO HAPPEN, UNCLE. WE WERE BOUND TO BE DISCOVERED!
27

WELL, I MUST ADMIT, YOU BOYS WERE CLEVER TO FIND OUT ABOUT THIS PHENOMENON OF NATURE RIGHT HERE ON MY PROPERTY!
YES, NATURE PROVIDED THIS CAVERN AND I ADDED TO IT!
ITO, DIVE BACK AND FETCH MAYOR MALLET, CHIEF McNAB, AND EDITOR PENBINDER AROUND TO THE FRONT DOOR... THE REST OF US WILL USE THE PASSAGE-WAY.

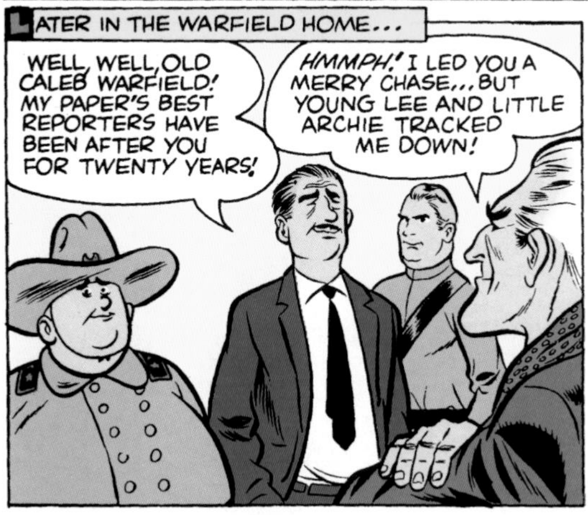
LATER IN THE WARFIELD HOME...
WELL, WELL, OLD CALEB WARFIELD! MY PAPER'S BEST REPORTERS HAVE BEEN AFTER YOU FOR TWENTY YEARS!
HMMPH! I LED YOU A MERRY CHASE... BUT YOUNG LEE AND LITTLE ARCHIE TRACKED ME DOWN!

JIMMY, I KNEW YOU'D MAKE A GOOD REPORTER THE MOMENT YOU TOLD ME OF THE OLD LADY—
YOU DID NOT! YOU CALLED HIM A WEDGE-HEAD...
SHH!

GENTLEMEN, SO THAT THEY'LL BE NO HARD FEELINGS TOWARDS ME FOR MY LITTLE ADVENTURE, I'M TURNING OVER TO THE TOWN OF RIVERDALE THE ENTIRE TREASURE THAT MY NEW FOUND MAP WILL LEAD US TO!

NOW, IF YOU WILL EXCUSE ME, I SHALL RETIRE TO MY STUDY, CHECK ALL MY MAPS AND LOCATE THE EXACT SPOT OF THE TREASURE!
28

SOON
WELL, UNCLE?
YES, I'VE LOCATED THE WHEREABOUTS OF THE TREASURE!
SPLENDID! AS MAYOR I MUST SAY THE TOWN IS PROUD OF YOU!

WHERE IS IT?
NOT FAR FROM HERE, ON AN ISLAND QUITE EASY TO REACH!

IT'S MANHATTAN ISLAND IN NEW YORK CITY!
NEW YORK!? WHERE ALL THOSE TALL BUILDINGS ARE?!

YES, AND THE EXACT LOCATION OF CAPTAIN LASHMAST'S BURIED TREASURE IS RIGHT UNDER SUCH A BUILDING... THE EMPIRE STATE BUILDING!

WELL, THE TOWN LOSES THAT TREASURE!
YES, GONE FOR GOOD NOW!
NICE TRY, THOUGH, WARFIELD... WARFIELD?
UNCLE?
29

TRACK 4 NEW YORK EXPRESS
THE END?

Archie
-IN-
"SINGIN' IN THE RAIN"
ARCHIE! SURELY YOU'RE NOT GOING OUT IN THAT TORRENTIAL DOWNPOUR?!!
LAST FEW DAYS OF SUMMER VACATION, MOM! I'M NOT GONNA SPEND IT COOPED UP IN THE HOUSE!

THE GANG WILL ALL BE AT POP'S AND I'M GONNA JOIN 'EM!

MISERY LOVES COMPANY! WE'LL ALL SPEND IT TOGETHER, SOBBING IN OUR SODAS!
TSK! CRAZY KIDS!
1

IT'S NOT FAIR TO RAIN ON OUR FINAL DAYS OF FREEDOM!

WE OUGHTA GET A "RAIN CHECK" FOR SPOILED VACATION DAYS!
POP'S

HAH! I KNEW THEY'D ALL BE ... HEY! WHERE'S OL' RON? SHE ISN'T HERE!
SHE BETTER NOT HEAR YOU CALLING HER OL' RON!
POP

WHATEVER! IT'S NOT LIKE HER TO MISS THIS GATHERING OF THE GLUM!!

ER- DON'T BE TOO HASTY, LAD! I DO BELIEVE SHE'S ABOUT TO MAKE AN ENTRANCE!
2

WELL! HELLO, FELLOW MOURNERS!

HEY! POP WAS RIGHT! THAT'S AN ENTRANCE!
SNAP!

YOU BOYS APPROVE OF MY RAINY DAY ATTIRE?
POP'S MENU

LET THEM GET THEIR EYES BACK IN THEIR HEADS, RON, BEFORE THEY ANSWER THAT!
IS IT TOO MUCH?
POP'S MENU

IT JUST SEEMED APPROPRIATE FOR A LATE, SUMMER SHOWER!
ANY SEASON OF THE YEAR, LUV! ...ANY SEASON!!

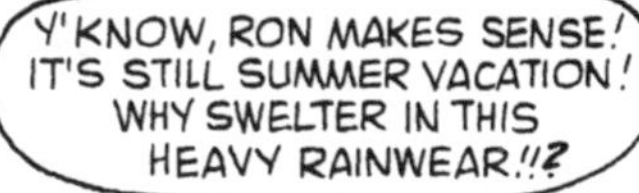
Y'KNOW, RON MAKES SENSE! IT'S STILL SUMMER VACATION! WHY SWELTER IN THIS HEAVY RAINWEAR!!?

RIGHT! I'M WITH YOU!
3

MEET YOU BACK HERE IN TWENTY MINUTES!
YEAH! WHAT ARE WE? SUGAR PLUMS? GONNA MELT IN A LITTLE PRECIPITATION?
POP'S

HAH! I TOLD YOU IT WAS TOO WET OUT, YOU SILLY BOY!!
GOTTA HURRY, MOM!

ARCHIE!! WHAT THE...?

OUR NEW, SUMMER RAINWEAR, FOLKS! ... ADIOS!!

(SIGH!) - EVERY GENERATION GETS WACKIER AND WACKIER!
-AND I USED TO THINK WE WERE THE SILLIEST TEEN-AGERS EVER!

HEY! EVERYBODY'S GETTING INTO THE ACT!
WE GOTTA LIVE OUR VACATION DAYS TO THE HILT!
4

HOW GREAT CAN IT GET?
WE'RE SINGIN' AND DANCIN' IN THE RAIN!

HEY! I LOVE IT!
ME, TOO! RAIN IS BEAUTIFUL!!

WE'RE ENDING OUR SUMMER VACATION WITH A SPLASH!
HA! ONLY WAY TO GO!!

...AND...
HMM? SO MANY MISSING ON OPENING DAY OF SCHOOL, MS. GRUNDY! WHAT HAPPENED?
SOME SORT OF EPIDEMIC OF VERY BAD COLDS, BOSS! MUST HAVE BEEN THOSE ROTTEN RAINS WE'VE BEEN HAVING!
PRINCIPAL
END

Archie in The Cape Caper

HI, FELLOWS! ANYBODY SEE JUGHEAD?
WHAT THE?
?

HA! HA! HEE! HAW! WHAT GARAGE SALE DID YOU FIND THAT STAR-SPANGLED UNDERWEAR?
HMPF!

WE DON'T HAVE A PHONE BOOTH FOR YOU TO CHANGE IN--- HOW ABOUT A BROOM CLOSET?

YOU GUYS WILL BE LAUGHING OUT OF THE OTHER SIDE OF YOUR MOUTHS WHEN I WIN FIRST PRIZE IN BETTY'S COSTUME!

HEY, CAPTAIN KLUTZ! HOW COME YOU'RE NOT FLYING?
POW!
POP!

RATS! THOSE GUYS UPSET ME SO, I FORGOT TO GET GAS!
CHUG! CHUG!
WHEEEZE!
2

WELL, WHAT DO WE HAVE HERE?
UH, I'M OUT OF GAS, OFFICER!
214

YOU SHOULDN'T HAVE ANY PROBLEM! WHY DON'T YOU CARRY YOUR CAR TO THE NEAREST GAS STATION?
EVERY-BODY THINKS THEY'RE A COMEDIAN!

THE COMIC CONVENTION IS NEARBY! I'LL WALK THE REST OF THE WAY!

UH, OH! THOSE KIDS WOULD GIVE ME A HARD TIME FOR SURE! --- I'LL JUST CUT THROUGH THE LOT!

WHEW! I'VE BEEN PRACTICING ON THIS MINI-TRAMPOLINE ALL DAY!

I THINK I'LL TAKE A BREAK!
3

RATS! I KEEP GETTING MY CAPE STUCK ON THESE BRANCHES!

WHOOOA!

YIPE!
BOY, THAT WAS A TERRIFIC HAUL!

HOLY COW! I DON'T BELIEVE THIS!
SPRONG!

CRASH!
4

GEE, I'M SORRY, SIR!

HEY! THAT'S THE DAYLIGHT BURGLAR!
?

CONGRATULATIONS! THERE'S A REWARD OUT FOR THIS JOKER!
THERE IS?

SAY! ARE YOU SOME KIND OF A NUT, OR ARE YOU REALLY A CAPED CRUSADER?
IT'S A LONG STORY, OFFICER!

OH, ARCHIE! WE'RE SO PROUD OF YOU!
AND HE'S GETTING ANOTHER $500 WHEN HE APPEARS ON THE JOHNNY MARSON SHOW!
PSST, BETTY! DO YOU THINK YOU CAN MAKE ME ONE OF THOSE COSTUMES?
DAILY BLAH
CAPED TEEN NABS CAT BURGLAR $500
END

Veronica in TALE OF ROW

GEE, WHAT'S WRONG? YOU SOUND ANGRY!
WEARY IS MORE LIKE IT!

LATELY, OUR DATES HAVE BEEN TOO STRENUOUS!

HUH? WHAT DO YOU MEAN? I THOUGHT YOU LIKED BEING OUTDOORS THIS TIME OF YEAR!

I DO! BUT THIS EXERCISE ROUTINE IS WEARING ME DOWN!

"LAST WEEK IT WAS SKATING..."
C'MON, RON! CATCH UP!
2

"...THE OTHER DAY IT WAS TENNIS..."

I NEED A REST!

IN SHORT, NO MORE EXERCISE FOR A WHILE, OR *NO MORE DATES!*
GULP!

GEE, RON, I DIDN'T REALIZE OUR RELATIONSHIP WAS BECOMING SO STRAINED!

HEY! I HAVE A RELAXING IDEA FOR TOMORROW! LET ME SURPRISE YOU!
OKAY!
3

THE NEXT DAY...
SEE! I PACKED US A PICNIC LUNCH! I'M GOING TO ROW OUT TO MATTIGAN'S ISLAND!

IT'S A LONG, HARD ROW, BUT IT'LL BE WORTH IT! LET'S GET STARTED!

THIS IS A NICE IDEA, ARCHIE!
PUFF! PUFF! THANKS! IT'LL BE A TOTALLY RESTFUL AND RELAXING DATE FOR YOU!

LATER ON THE ISLAND...
THIS WAS A WONDERFUL DATE, ARCHIE!
THANKS! BUT NOW IT'S TIME TO START BACK!

YOU JUST ENJOY THE SUNSET WHILE I ROW BACK!
OKAY! YOU'RE THE BOSS!
4

OUCH!
ARCHIE! WHAT'S WRONG?

I-I GOT A SPLINTER IN MY HAND WHEN I GRABBED THE OAR!
LET ME SEE! OOOH! IT'S A BIG ONE AND IT'S IN DEEP!

YOU WON'T BE ABLE TO GET IT OUT UNTIL WE GET BACK HOME!
B-BUT HOW WILL I ROW LIKE THIS?

YOU CAN'T ROW! IT'LL BE TOO PAINFUL... OH NO!!
GULP!

OOMPH! UGH! GRRR... SOME DATE THIS TURNED OUT TO BE!
END

Archie IN PRE-SCHOOL JITTERS
HIRING STUDENTS TO HELP GET THE BUILDING READY FOR THE START OF SCHOOL WAS A GOOD IDEA!
HMM...
EVENTS

I'M NOT SO SURE OF THAT!
THAT CARTON OF STUDY SHEETS BELONGS IN THE SCIENCE ROOM, ARCHIE!
YES, SIR!

HI, MS. GRUNDY, MR. WEATHERBEE!
BEING HERE LETS STUDENTS PREPARE THEMSELVES FOR A NEW SCHOOL YEAR!
HI, ARCHIE!
WHOA!
SLIP!
SPLASH!
KLUNK!
FLOP!
CRASH!
ARCHIE?
I'M ALL RIGHT, SIR! I JUST HAD A LITTLE ACCIDENT!
HEH, HEH! I'LL HAVE EVERYTHING CLEANED UP IN A JIFFY!
SIGH! OKAY, ARCHIE!
2

DON'T LOOK AT ME LIKE THAT! THE STUDENTS REALLY ARE PREPARING THEMSELVES FOR THE START OF SCHOOL!
AH-HA!
THINK OF DEALING WITH ARCHIE AS PREPARATION FOR THE BEGINNING OF YOUR SCHOOL YEAR!
OH! THANKS!
POP'S
LATER ON THE SECOND FLOOR...
OKAY, ARCHIE! HELP ME VASH DESE VINDOWS!
RIGHT, MR. SVENSON!
HEE, HEE! FIRST CLOSE DE VINDOW!
OOPS!
THAT'S FUNNY! I THOUGHT I FELT A RAINDROP!
SPLOOSH!
AHH!
3

WHAT THE...? A SPONGE? ARCHIE ANDREWS!!
S-SORRY, MR. WEATHERBEE! IT WAS AN ACCIDENT!
YAH! IT VAS AN ACCIDENT!

WHEW!
WELL...OKAY! OKAY!

LATER STILL...
ARCHIE, RUN THESE FOOTBALL JERSEYS THROUGH OUR NEW WASHER!
YES, SIR, COACH CLAYTON!
RHS
MAKE SURE YOU PUT IN ENOUGH SOAP! THIS IS AN INDUSTRIAL-SIZE WASHER!
WOW! IT SURE IS BIG!
SUPER-SUDIZER
I GUESS TWO BOXES OF SOAP SHOULD BE ENOUGH!
TIDAL WAVE
TIDAL
4

HI, COACH! HOW'S EVERYTHING GOING?
IF YOU MEAN HOW'S ARCHIE DOING...
LAUND ROOM

...HE'S IN THERE WASHING...
YEOW!
BOOM!
BANG!
KA-SLOOSH!

WHAT IN THE WORLD...
FIZZ

D-DON'T WORRY! I'M OKAY! I GUESS I OVERLOADED THE WASHER!
GULP! IT'S NO USE!

SCHOOL IS ABOUT TO OPEN BUT I'M JUST NOT READY TO DEAL WITH ARCHIE YET!
ARRG!
COACH
THE END